Bea in The Nutcracker

Rachel Isadora

Nancy Paulsen Books 🌀 **An Imprint of Penguin Group (USA)**

For Gillian

NANCY PAULSEN BOOKS
Published by the Penguin Group
Penguin Group (USA) LLC
375 Hudson Street
New York, NY 10014

USA | Canada | UK | Ireland | Australia
New Zealand | India | South Africa | China
penguin.com
A Penguin Random House Company

Library of Congress Cataloging-in-Publication Data is available upon request.
Manufactured in China by RR Donnelley Asia Printing Solutions Ltd.
ISBN 978-0-399-25231-0
1 3 5 7 9 10 8 6 4 2

Design by Marikka Tamura.
Text set in Rosemary.
The illustrations were done with pencil, ink, and oil paint on paper.

The Nutcracker is a ballet.
It tells the story of a little girl
named Clara who is given
a Nutcracker for Christmas.
She loves him so much that
she falls asleep with him in
her arms. That night,
she dreams fantastic dreams . . .

Here is Bea. She is excited because her ballet class is going to perform **The Nutcracker.**

She will be Clara!

Sam will be the Nutcracker who turns into the Prince.

These are the costumes the dancers will wear.

snowflake

Candy Cane

party guests

Sugar Plum Fairy

flower

mouse

soldier

"Tie your ribbons tight!"
says Ms. Nancy.
"The curtain is about
to go up."

The music starts,
and the show begins.

Clara and her friends receive presents.

Clara loves her Nutcracker.

When the party is over,
Clara falls asleep with
her Nutcracker.

She dreams that the Nutcracker turns into a real soldier.

Suddenly, scary mice appear.

The Nutcracker calls
his soldiers into battle.

The Nutcracker and his soldiers win the battle!

He is really a Prince, and
he invites Clara to his kingdom,
the Land of Sweets.

The snowflakes twirl to welcome them.

The flowers waltz.

**The Sugar Plum Fairy
waves her wand, and . . .**

the Candy Cane leaps into the air!

jingle jingle

jingle jingle

jingle jingle

jingle jingle

Clara thanks everyone for a wonderful time.

The ballet is over.

clap clap clap
clap clap clap

Hooray!

clap clap clap

It is time for the dancers to take a bow.

clap **clap** clap

Bravo!

clap clap **clap**

Backstage, there
are cupcakes.
"This reminds me of
the Land of Sweets!"
says Sam.

"But these are real!" says Bea.

Before she leaves, Bea gives the Nutcracker a hug. "Merry Christmas!" she whispers.